DARK KNIGHT

THE ANTICHRIST OR JUST ANOTHER MADMAN?

ROGER ELWOOD

Creation House
Lake Mary, Florida

Creation House
Strang Communications Company
600 Rinehart Road
Lake Mary, FL 32746
(407) 333-0600

*To those fighting
the Saad Nasurs
of this world*

ACKNOWLEDGMENTS

Praise God that 1990 was a year of substantial turning points for me, and virtually all of them centered on my career.

It was the year I started work on the sequel to *Angelwalk*, titled *Fallen Angel*, which has gone on to outsell the original book. Then I wrote another novel titled *Children of the Furor*, dealing with one of the critical issues of our time: the rise of the skinhead neo-Nazi movement. These were joined by books in which the laboratory use of animals, the commercialization of the church and various other topics had their places as pivotal plot elements.

It was also the year that saw the beginning of my relationship with Creation House, the publisher of *Dwellers*. I have come to know them as a group of warm and dedicated brothers and sisters in Christ.

Quite a year indeed!

My association with Creation House continues here with a book that shows that the spirit of Adolf Hitler, Josef Stalin and other senseless tyrants of the twentieth century lives on in the person of Saddam Hussein.

Dark Knight isn't essentially about Hussein, at least not directly, although many readers will take it that way. It is about his type of individual, someone either fully possessed by Satan or else a very willing puppet of the Prince of Darkness — someone quite capable of bringing the rest of the world down around him if necessary in a perverse kind of victory that only he could consider somehow glorious.

Despite the conclusion of the Gulf War in 1991, you can be sure that this volatile region will someday prove the birthplace of yet another human tragedy, another madman. It is, after all, where Armageddon will take place.

Even from the beginning the Middle East has been notable for the astonishing impact of the events that have occurred there.

Where Adam and Eve lost Eden.

Where Cain slew Abel.

Where so many apostles lost their lives to crucifixion or decapitation or some other horrible means of execution.

Where the Iranians held captive so many Americans for so long.

It is where a street cry of "Death to America!" is an unrelenting chant as well as a mind-set.

Where the Islamic religion holds sway over tens of millions of compliant followers, people so blinded by the evil leaders to whom they look for guidance that many of them end up being demonized with an unspeakable blood lust and the fiercest malevolence toward anyone from the outside world.

INTRODUCTION

Biblical prophecy is never more fascinating than when we suppose it is being fulfilled right before our eyes. But then past generations have thought that innumerable times, only to be disappointed.

The fault must lie with either prophecy itself or those who build their lives around some preconceived manifestation of prophecy. I, for one, will opt for placing the blame on fallible human nature and its expectations rather than the prophetic utterances of Spirit-led prophets, whose words are actually the Lord's since they wrote under His guidance to give us His inerrant Word.

There is more to prophecy than strictly the end-times

portion of it, though this has captured a lion's share of attention — and understandably so in an age that seems bent on learning what the future holds, resorting to astrology and divining crystals as well as Ouija boards, tarot cards and whatever else might be used. In the Bible we have the books of Ezekiel and Daniel and Isaiah, many of whose prophecies already have come to pass, as well as Revelation, which points to a future not as yet realized. All are intertwined into a symbiotic whole, and it is that whole that must be studied to its fullest, including those prophecies no longer "current."

Generally, it must be admitted that the bulk of biblical prophecy points in one direction — the time of Christ's second coming and what lies beyond this epochal moment in future history. And all of it is centered in one region and one region only.

The Middle East.

It is here that Christianity was born.

It is here that Saddam Hussein and egomaniacal puppets like him are continually going to be unleashing their hatred toward Christians and Jews, indeed toward anyone who stands in the way of their military and Islamic outlook, both bent on conquering the world.

It has been my desire not just to do a book that repeats the news content of what 1991 brought us. It is instead my commitment to delve into the mind-set of a Middle Eastern despot very much like Saddam Hussein to see why he is the way he is and to try to find out if there is any decency, any compassion, left in him. The man who smiles as he balances a child on his knee is the same one who orders the nerve-gas slaughter of thousands of his own people.

We do two things by looking at such a man with the starkest clarity. For we are then brought face-to-face with someone who is as much like Satan the deceiver as any human being can be. No mortal flesh can assume all the characteristics of the devil. But Hussein and Hitler and others have come as close as we will ever be able to see on this sin-ravaged planet.

But there is something else I intend; that is, to prepare the reader who picks up *Dark Knight*.

For what?

Not what — but whom.

The next tyrant from the Middle East who is ready to take center stage right behind Saddam Hussein.

AUTHOR'S NOTE

I should prepare the reader for the format I've utilized for the following material. The essential narrator is a journalist on the run. He has been compiling incriminating evidence against the Dark Knight.

Surrounding him are soldiers and undercover espionage people from the Western governments that have agreed to protect him. As the book opens, he is alone, fearful, in the process of looking over news clips, interview transcripts, pilfered portions of Saad Nasur's diary, and other bits and pieces that will form the basis of the book he is writing.

You, the reader, are looking over his shoulder as he goes through piles of all this, deciding what to use and what to exclude. So you will be reading not a straight-line narrative but rather the pieces of a mosaic in the same way a journalist would be reading.

Much of what you find will be fact — masquerading as fiction. And quite a bit will be maximally controversial, particularly those portions dealing with Islam, the German government and certain individuals within American government and industry who have been on the take for many years, thereby explaining how the real Saddam Hussein through the façade of the fictional Saad Nasur could have gotten all his munitions, all his chemicals, all those deadly viruses and such without anyone's smelling a rat, as the expression goes.

Thank you for your interest in reading *Dark Knight* and for your attention as you encounter a literary attempt to do things just a bit differently.

PROLOGUE

I look over his notes, as his publisher, and I find myself filled with admiration for this, my author, but also my friend. I read his comments to me in scattered little notes, those sticky kind that will cling to anything, and I try to piece together what he will not be able to finish.

I sit so safely in my penthouse office, with all my sophisticated communications equipment, and I realize that I was, in the end, able to give him so little.

I leaf through the manuscript, in its various bits and pieces, trying to decide how to bring the great-

est coherence to what he left behind — adding a few paragraphs of my own and hoping I catch the essence of my friend as well as he deserved.

My name is Mouphas Fakarian.

I once was a Muslim. I stopped being a Muslim after piecing together the contents you are about to read.

Yes, that is quite true. I worshipped Allah in spirit and in fact. I was willing to sacrifice my life for Islam. I carried the Koran with me everywhere.

I considered any other faith blasphemous. Those who were Christians or Jews were infidels, less worthy than dung on the farms of my land.

Only Islam came from Allah.

Only Islam was blessed by Allah.

But in time I saw what was happening to those who had

been my Muslim brothers and sisters.

I saw their hatred.

I saw their desire for vengeance against any who disagreed with them.

And this all came about because of and through one man. Saad Nasur.

Some time ago, before I realized Saad Nasur deserved a curse rather than a tribute, before I had gathered very much material together, I intended to do this work to honor him. You see, I believed everything the Islamic press said about him as well as my own impressions of him during our various earlier meetings.

Saad is the Son of Allah — God....

That was when I became uneasy.

They could call Saad Nasur a great man. They could say he was the greatest indeed since Mohammed. They could point to him as the modern savior of the Arab peoples. They could do all of this and more, but they could never refer to him as a god and expect this journalist to be supportive. Nor use the Koran or any other part of Islam as justification.

In this his influence was blatantly similar to that which allowed Adolf Hitler to captivate the German people. Granted that the Germans are an historically war-like tribe, if I may refer to them in that manner; but nothing in their past could give rise to any hint of the barbarity into which Hitler led them. He seems to have been so powerful as to rob them of any will of their own, getting them to throw aside even basic human decency, generosity, kindness — those elements that help to separate man from the animals.

Saad Nasur used the same gambit, shall we say.

Anti-Semitism.

He built up within my people an all-consuming malevolence toward the Jews. He blamed Zionism for many ills, though the *logic* of so much of what he expounded should have been notable for its sheer absence. But then who could have seriously blamed *only* the Jews for the German economic collapse in the decade prior to World War II? It was just that the Jews were so visible, prominent in banking and other circles, and undoubtedly guilty of *some* of the avarice of which they were accused.

(You see how these attitudes linger in me even now, when I should find them unspeakable.)

The *kikes*, as Saad Nasur called them, were consumed by a desire to punish any Arab nation that showed pronounced sympathy for the Palestinians. They knew of the Nazi seeds within the Ba'ath Party, and they were determined to destroy Saad's country — my country — or so he had us believe.

It wasn't such a giant step for him to cut us loose from our Islamic moorings, at least enough to get us to accept the possibility of his divinity.

Saad, the Son of Allah....

Even the cynics and skeptics among us — the journalists — began to wonder: Could it be that he is indeed Allah in the flesh, that after so many centuries we finally have our own incarnation, Christians no longer possessing a monopoly in a matter such as this?

I could have been convinced of this, despite my early reticence, if the record bore out any possibility, even the remotest, that this was so.

The record did nothing of the sort, as you shall see.

The God I now worship, the Allah I once did — neither could be personified in the form of this egomaniacal barbarian. For my God, while no stranger to wrath, is also a God of forgiveness, of blessing, of compassion. My God sent His Son to die for me.

It would be no different with Saad Nasur if he were a god, but a god without the love embodied in Jehovah. He would still murder his own family if that served his purposes. He would personally administer the poison or plunge the dagger or aim the pistol if he felt like it at any given moment to rid himself of anyone who displeased him.

It has not been easy throwing away my hopes about this

man. It has not been easy giving up the dream of liberation that he provided all of us. It has not been easy watching my idol crumble to ashes and dust at my feet.

I tremble as I think of the change in him.

No!

That is not it. He has always been the same, from his childhood years to the present.

I remember when he told me about his school days during one of our interviews.

"I used to carry a loaded revolver with me," he had said. "My family and I were very poor at the time. The poor were victimized in those days. I used the revolver as a statement. I was saying, 'I am not like the other poor. Step on my toes, and you will find a bullet in your heart before the sun sets.'"

There are others who comprehend what Saad Nasur really was. That is, in the Islamic community.

It was not news to those in the West who had seen this reality ever since he invaded another Muslim country. Yet many of us, as Islamic brothers, ignored what the blood on his hands should have told us, the blood of men and women in that violated land, men and women who tried to resist him but were shot to death or bombed or blown up by land mines.

Including his own soldiers.

"Deserters will die!" he declared.

And they did, by the thousands.

But nothing more clearly gets to the core of Saad Nasur than when he ordered the slaughter of babies as an act of terror in the brother country he had invaded.

Soldiers entered the nurseries of various hospitals and clinics and turned off the oxygen feeding into scores of incubators. Even so, some did not die. Seeing this, soldiers opened the incubators and speared the surviving babies with bayonets.

There was glee on the faces of these men, though I call them that with more than a little reluctance.

I came across the photographs by accident. They were

slipped to me by a member of one of the soldiers' families. A note attached to them read:

See what Saad Nasur has done to my son. See that ghastliness to which my boy has been driven. Can this foul thing be the product of my womb, the one to whom I have given so much love, now a wild beast stalking the innocent, the helpless?

And, yes, I saw.

I saw the expression on his face, the wide eyes, the open mouth, the passion, the enjoyment, the blood lust.

Over the children!

As soon as I regained control of my emotions, I read the rest of what that woman had written:

My little Rashid, sweet, sweet Rashid, had been so kind when he was younger. He brought home birds and nursed them back to health, then let them go, to be free, as Allah intended. He loved his grandmother. He waited on her every need. When we were at war with our neighbor, and he was still too young to fight, he became the man of the house while his father went off to battle. Rashid was wonderful, kind and brave and loving. But now a mad animal comes home to me with the blood of infants on his hands!

I came into possession of many scraps of this sort of evidence. They fell into place, like pieces from the pit of

19

hell, to complete an infernal puzzle. What I saw was a nightmare. What I saw was a man but not a man, a messiah but not a messiah, a human being but not one at all.

And now I find myself hiding out.

I have everything I need together now, and it will soon be picked up by a special courier dispatched by my American publisher. Eventually a book will come off the presses to be distributed worldwide.

Saad Nasur is trying to stop me.

Saad Nasur is trying to stop anyone who might have a part in the birth of this book.

I have no freedom of movement, none whatsoever.

The sympathetic governments shielding me at various times must station a number of heavily armed guards around the clock for the foreseeable future, not to mention the dogs, to ensure my survival. Perhaps they will have to do so for the rest of my life.

Dogs! To help keep my former Muslim brothers from murdering me!

This material I am presenting comes from a variety of sources: from the personal journal of Saad Nasur as well as letters written by his minister of diplomacy and various witnesses to the atrocities of the Ba'ath regime, including reports from environmental agencies.

To me much was given, and therefore much was required. I was allowed *inside* Saad Nasur, in a figurative sense. And if I were to betray him, I was warned, I would forfeit my life — in the most painful manner possible.

It was with that understanding that he turned over to me his diary, letters, little pieces of paper upon which he had scribbled thoughts.

I was surprised by how literate a man Saad Nasur proved to be, how intelligent. Not that, in those days of adulation, I ever considered him stupid. But there was something else I had not expected to discover, a certain sophistication, an ability to write with distinctive style and, sometimes, an almost lyrical quality.

So I would not be surprised if what you are about to read surprises you rather substantially, changing at least some of your conceptions about this fiend, this beast.

Did I say that I was once a Muslim? Yes, of course I did. I had embraced the precepts of the great Mohammed most of my life.

I started to change, but not after hordes fell on the bloody fields of battle in and around my country. Somehow I could tolerate that, given the nature of warfare.

It was the innocent, yes, the unsuspecting, the helpless, the uninvolved — their bodies lifeless reminders of one man's unrestrained madness.

No, I did not think Saad Nasur insane when soldiers fell. If that were so, then Montgomery, Churchill, Roosevelt, Eisenhower and MacArthur would have to be judged in like manner.

Rather I thought him so when babies died of suffocation, when children were torn in half by exploding bombs, when the elderly were reduced to bone fragments by buildings toppling over on them, when people gasped away their lives through the inhalation of poisons manufactured in Germany and shipped to my country via clandestine routes that evaded the stringent safeguards against any of this happening.

When the seagulls could not fly.

Ah, yes, that was when I thought him insane.

Following is an excerpt I ran across in a recent issue of the International Geographic Society bulletin. My heart was heavy as I read it, for I myself saw this very image time and time again. Perhaps you, my reader, remember seeing such pictures on television, or you may have read this very account.

EDITOR'S PAGE

The gull was dying, its body covered by a thick black substance that oozed onto its feathers and through to the skin, subjecting the bird to slow suffocation; and if it didn't somehow make land, it would drown, the water that had been so good to it, the water that gave it food, now its place of burial; but even if it managed, in a floppy and anguished manner to wade through the heavy liquid and stumble up on shore, there still was no hope for this hapless creature, its lungs starved for air, air that was blocked by one stretch of fifty million barrels of oil, its eyes soon blinded so that it would smash pitiably against rocks again and again until, stunned, and even more confused, it could only sit down without moving further, surrounded by an all-encompassing darkness punctuated by vague, fleeting images that managed to be seen in the midst of near-total blindness; and somewhere in its little brain was an image of a nest, and three tiny figures, their mouths open as they anticipated their mother's return, and, soon, without the food she had been trying to provide, would die as well, leaning back against that intricately woven nest, and closing eyes that were hardly open in the first place, their tiny, tiny lungs collapsing, their feet jerking in final spasms a few times, and then gone, gone like their mother who took in a deep breath, trying one last time to survive, and then, the odor of oil dank through her pin-point nostrils, she sighed, not knowing in her dumbness what had happened, and was gone.

When I read those words, I wept. I wept because of the images they projected, but also for the implication beyond the words. Let me tell you about the writer of that poignant passage. His name is Clyde Holmes.

Before writing what he did, he was a man who did not believe in evil. He believed in the potential meanness of human nature, yes. He knew that people were capable of loathsome acts. But he was not alive during World War II. He was born decades later. His only awareness of the Nazi atrocities came from old news footage and television mini-series and magazine photo spreads, not personal experience as with so many of us.

I myself remember standing outside· Dachau one chilly afternoon after the camp had been liberated. Wave after wave of survivors, skeleton-like figures, emerged, most of whom had to be helped into awaiting vehicles which would take them to hospitals. Many would die in those hospitals, but at least they would die as free men and women and children.

There was no mortal liberation of any kind for the piles of bodies in a ditch around the camp.

Clyde Holmes never experienced precisely that evil or rather that result of evil. He never smelled the awful odor of decay. He never vomited from the sight. He never talked to the soldiers given the job of gathering together the remains, a task that would come back to haunt them years later at night as they screamed in horror.

Many years later Clyde Holmes saw birds die, saw marine mammals die; so it would seem obvious that he was spared the worst results of men without the loving and true Creator.

Oh no, he wasn't.

He saw skies blackened by the smoke from hundreds of oil well fires. He saw a once orderly country, a prospering country turned into a kind of literal hell, for how has hell been depicted over the centuries if not as a black and foul place with continual flames, people crying in misery, all sense of hope drained from them?

It is interesting that the madman who left all this behind also had been called a devil, and rightly so.

A devil bent on recreating the hell of his own master.

A hell of poisonous air destined to spawn tuberculosis, blood disease, cancer, blindness.

For the current generation.

For the next.

A hell of the bodies of children with no heads because troops either followed the orders of their commander-in-chief or gave in to their own hideous desires.

A hell of women sobbing because they had been raped repeatedly.

A hell that Clyde Holmes had no idea ever existed, evil beyond mere human nature itself.

He believes now.

Clyde Holmes believes.

He has seen the fruits of evil. And though he has long since left this place of torment, it stays with him — how could it not?

M_ouphas Fakarian here...._

Whatever the original vision of Saad Nasur had been, there was no measure of it left, unless he had intended to do what he did from the beginning, the corruption of it there at the start.

What he did to that little country, he planned to duplicate elsewhere. He planned to destroy England and rebuild it in his image.

"The English seem so righteous," he reportedly said. "But they aren't. Look at what they did in India. Just stop a moment and examine the slaughter there, the one that got Gandhi off his holy mount. Has anyone ever come down on them as the world has on me? I mean, can't I be allowed a little massacre from time to time without being called all manner of terrible names?"

A deserting general gave me a file of papers, including maps, diagrams and memorandums that detailed what he intended to do to the English.

"No infidel monument shall be allowed to stand!" Saad supposedly said during a war council meeting.

That included Saint Paul's and Westminster Abbey and cathedrals throughout the country.

All were to be leveled to the ground.

Any citizens caught worshipping inside should be executed immediately — in the sanctuary itself as a blood offering to Allah!

"Are we to cut the women and children in half?" a subordinate was said to have asked.

"Most assuredly," Saad replied.

"I realize this has been attempted before," Saad told me. "They will think that no one will try it again. They will think that other men have learned their lesson and that no one will be so foolish as to ignore what history taught.

"That is their failing. They think we look at defeat and it retards us, that we cower in fear at what happened to other mighty armies. But we look at defeat only as a means of learning victory. We will not be so open this time. We will bribe more officials. We will get our armaments in total secrecy. And when they think us most quiet, most compliant, we will spring like a lion and devour them all!"

Saad said he most wanted to get his hands on the current prime minister of England and his predecessor.

"They will be led into the center of Trafalgar Square," he said, drawing me closer, "and be shot by my dozen finest men, and their bodies will remain there for all to see!"

He was exuberant at that thought.

"And next the queen! And after that — !"

He stopped abruptly as he saw my look of shock.

"Are you so sensitive, Mr. Journalist?" he said sneeringly. "Can you not stand that which gives me pleasure? I want to be certain you will convey accurately what it is that, as they say these days, turns me on."

He took hold of my lapels and shook me.

"If you cannot do that, I will have both your hands cut off!"

He continued staring at me.

"Will you do what I say, Mr. Journalist?"

I nodded.

"I want to *hear* you say it!" he demanded.

"Yes," I told him, "yes, I will do as you say."

"Exactly?"

"To the final comma and period," I answered.

He released me then, pleased that I had bowed to him, but not knowing my thoughts. Not realizing what I intended to do.

To follow God or man....

I had made my choice. And I was prepared to die for it.

The following transcript was taken specifically from a tape recording made by Saad Nasur which was found in his underground bunker.

—M.F

The bunker is behind and below me just now. As I record this, I am standing for a moment above ground. In the distance I see bright lights in the sky, bursting briefly, then gone, like phantom stars.

And, yes, I do think in such terms, though my enemies would have it otherwise.

Earlier this evening I stood on this very spot with Mokahr. My loyal Mokahr....

"Beautiful, is it not?" I said to him then, as I say everything, with no fear whatever of any possible rebuttal.

"Indeed it is," Mokahr replied with dutiful promptness. "A celebration!"

A puzzling thought struck me at that moment, and I turned to face him.

"Why is it that they call me a monster?" I suddenly asked this man who has been at my side for nearly twenty years. "Tell me the truth, Mokahr, or I will have your head delivered to me with a tangerine stuck in your mouth."

"The truth is that I cannot imagine why they call you a monster, or any such name," he told me, sincerity intent on his weathered face, crowned as it is by that pure white hair. "It remains a mystery that is quite beyond any probing."

My eyes narrowed as I pressed him further.

"The truth, absolutely?"

"Oh, yes, the truth, absolutely," he assured me.

I turned back toward the bunker.

"One other thing, Mokahr," I said as he looked at me questioningly. "I have asked it before: When are you going to give up your infidel beliefs and join the true faith?"

"If it be God's will, I would say quite soon," he answered

"Islam is God's will," I told him. "Do not ever forget that simple fact. Anything else is as dung under our feet, something to be scraped off with disgust because it smells so badly."

"As you say," he said quietly.

Although I abhor his religion, he is still one of the very few people I can trust. And I know, of course, that the best way to convince Mokahr is simply to keep after the man. I have no choice in the matter, you see. I must do that. I must keep after him day by day by day until he stands defiantly before his Christ and curses him with every blasphemy.

CLICK-CLICK. THE RECORDER IS SHUT OFF, AND SO IS SAAD NASUR — BUT ONLY FOR THAT INSTANT.

Mouphas Fakarian again....

Private moments with this man?

Of such there is a scarcity.

To say he had built a wall around himself is cliché, of course, but he certainly had done that. Although it had not been a physical wall, it might as well have been. For this wall was built upon fear — fear of death, fear of pain, fear of losing all of one's possessions.

Any individual to which Saad took a dislike was in danger.

Any individual who seemed to be in a position to threaten him was dealt with.

He controlled everyone around him.

And he made them like it.

He ridiculed them. He broke their egos into the tiniest pieces and superimposed his own instead.

And he made them like it.

He also used sex. He would take the wife of any of his cabinet members, at any given moment, and make her sleep with him. When the husband found out, he naturally would become enraged. But he would also value his life more than anything else.

And he made them like it.

He would rob the people he governed. He would dominate every aspect of their lives, giving them little freedom and wasting their money on armaments instead of available food and clothes and medicine.

And he made them like it.

Publisher's Note:

Having made it through Mouphas's manuscript to this point, I feel it necessary to break in. I am convinced my friend would agree if he were still able to.

You see, since Mouphas's death, information has come to light about just how much Saad Nasur robbed his people. I am now interpolating some of the material along these lines. Here are a few of the facts:

The Nasur clan, and they must be called that, skimmed 5 percent of all oil income for what were called "palace expenditures." That percentage over the years amounted to the equivalent of $10 to $12 billion! It was not only hidden away in Swiss bank accounts, but also invested in firms doing business in at least a dozen countries.

Including the United States!

Emmett Heddington, who has been called the leading detective in the world, told me personally that Saad Nasur owned pieces of two of the very defense contractors that manufactured a great deal of the military equipment used in the Allied offensive against him, which meant Saad made a profit on the deaths of his own soldiers. Hundreds of thousands of their bodies littered the desert of his native country, and yet at the same time he was counting the bottom-line dollars those two companies were taking in as a result.

Yes, that is truly shocking. But there is another fact that transcends it.

Five of the leading hawks in Congress were continuing to receive clandestine monies from a speakers' bureau that had been set up to camouflage any involvement on Saad's part, Heddington revealed. He also pointed out the bunker that was shelled by the Allies, which supposedly was only for civilian use.

Those five senators, Heddington said, had all received early tips about the military significance of it — the civilian aspect being just a convenient façade — and yet none of the senators spoke up. They easily could have prevented the slaughter but chose not to do so. One must ask the question of whether or not Saad Nasur paid them to keep quiet. And if that was the case, then what could his motivation have been?

The answer is obvious: to create an embarrassment for the United States. Heddington affirmed this as well.

Saad Nasur engineered the environment that led to the slaughter of innocent men, women and children.

And five U.S. senators aided and abetted him! Three were liberals. Two were conservatives. All of them had campaigned for political office on the basis of their strong patriotic values.

Yet, as it turns out, everything has had its price tag for these men, illegal and indeed immoral payments being a fact of life for them. Corruption wasn't endemic to one train of political thought, you can be sure.

Here is how it was done: They were booked for speaking engagements under contracts that specified they were to be paid anyway if the organization wanting them had to cancel for whatever reason. These five individuals had a flurry of alleged cancellations but kept the money — tens of thousands of dollars' worth!

And they kept their mouths shut.

Yes, the tentacles of Saad Nasur knew no boundaries.

The village on the edge of hell — that was what they called it. An appropriate name except that ultimately hell arose and gobbled up Al-Khari.

It was near a factory built to produce

germs for use against the Allied forces, and also Israel, who was not officially involved in the war. Many of the strains of various plagues were close to completion, ready to be loaded onto Azazi warheads and shot out of mobile launchers at the American, Egyptian, Syrian, British, Italian and Turkish troops.

Something went wrong.

Even though the strongest possible combination of Muslim artillery and missile units were grouped around the factory, seemingly able to intercept any attack, more than a thousand sorties got through, nevertheless, reducing it to a twisted pile of concrete and steel — and escaping germs.

Many of these died soon after exposure to the air. But most lasted long enough to make it on air currents into Al-Khari, infecting the inhabitants with diseases previously known as well as new diseases altogether unheard of by the worldwide medical communities.

No help could be given to the citizens of Al-Khari. None at all.

There was just no way exposure to the germs running rampant among them could be allowed to spread beyond that one spot.

According to my informed source, once the enemy military forces were destroyed, a decision was made by the Allies to destroy the village. It was burned by igniting chemicals that were designed to leave nothing behind, from microbes on up the scale

Following is the transcript of part of a report received by me on a shortwave transmission from one of the last villagers alive:

It is a terrible thing to see your family die before your eyes. It is a terrible thing to watch your sons and daughters gasping their lives away. It is a terrible thing to know you will join them soon and that Mohammed is doing nothing to help you. Mohammed has deserted us.

O Mohammed, where are you now?

I think that is yet another part of this, having our faith collapse in a heap at our feet along with those we love....

I cannot continue this communication much longer. I have something alive and squirming inside my stomach, something that is growing, working its way throughout my poor body....

I am thinking mad thoughts now. You can detect that, can you not? I am thinking that I want to put my hands around the throat of my supreme leader and squeeze the very life from him, as mine is being taken so cruelly from me.

"We trusted you," I would tell him. "We trusted you to bring us redemption, respect, power.

"You failed.

"And now we have only the ashes of our lives at our feet, and I step through these now into the dominion of death."

There were other reports similar to that one.

As a result of what happened to Al-Khari, Muslim leaders called once again for *jihad* — a holy war. Certainly the residents of Al-Khari once might have joined them, fighting for Allah.

They would have done anything for Allah and his messenger, the great Mohammed.

But then hell lapped them up in its maw and never, ever let go.

I had documented all of this, I thought, from a safe distance, receiving other shortwave transmissions which provided the glimpses I gave earlier.

There was just no way exposure to the germs running rampant among them could be allowed to spread beyond that one spot....

But it is one thing to say the germs could not be allowed to spread and quite another to realize that many were released *on purpose* by the Muslims as a last gasp of defiance.

I have now come to question their very humanity.

As the humanity of the Germans was questioned during and after World War II, so it will be when this atrocity by so-called men is examined in the months to follow.

But I will not be among those participating in the process. I don't know if even this brief communication will ever be released. Perhaps it will be destroyed by someone somewhere who decides it is not in the national interest for my words to be disseminated.

Because of who provided the germs in the first place.

Ah, that is the real tragedy here. Madmen will use any weapon you give to them. But perhaps the worst sin lies at the doorstep of those who dared to concoct the potion, so to speak.

I am dying because of just a single germ — for it takes no more than that to reach the bloodstream and play its havoc.

A single germ not even visible to the naked eye.

My mind is confused now. My heart is beating faster. I do not know what I am saying.

I must stop, for I haven't the energy to type anymore. Perhaps if I can escape this horrible place, I may survive. I must try. For the people I must try.

Here is a note from Saad Nasur to an aide.

—M.F

I read that report about Al-Khari. Do the
Americans expect me to surrender now?
I regret the loss, you know. The loss is
terrible. It is one that I shall not soon forget.
Yes, it is.
Those chemicals, those germs——I could have used
them.

M_ouphas Fakarian here again...._

Nothing you have read thus far does more than skim the surface of the evil that swarms around Saad Nasur — no, that is only part of the truth. Evil does encircle him, but it comes from within him as well.

I have heard him threaten awful things in the name of Allah. But nothing so monstrous as what he did to a family merely because the father, George Hawatmeh, his minister of oil exports, disagreed with him.

This transcript is taken from a group of tape recordings found in the salvaged personal belongings of George Hawatmeh. Nothing has been censored in any way.

Saad Nasur had the most penetrating eyes into which you could ever peer. He was not a bad-looking man, quite ruggedly built, endowed with health, a quick, intelligent mind and the ability to stir the masses.

That is what I saw in him early on, someone, as the Americans would say, to whom I should hitch my wagon. We got along from the very start, becoming friends when we were both just launching our political careers.

"I want our people to be proud," he told me as we sat on the veranda of his home one evening, the desert stretching out before us.

"So do I," was my response. "It has been too long that Muslims have lived in subjection to a foreign nation in one way or another," I told him. "To be free, free in the truest sense — that is my dream!"

I remember his next words as if they were spoken yesterday. "I want you to share the victory," he said. "Will you join me as my minister of oil exports?"

I thought for a few minutes about the implications of his request. It was obviously his intention to use oil as a weapon — and more besides. OPEC had tried a similar tactic in the 1970s, and I reminded him of this when I spoke again.

Saad Nasur agreed. "But they merely played with what I have in mind," he said. "When I say weapon, I mean it — not a powder puff with which to slap the infidels, but a dagger to plunge into their hearts!"

It disturbed me to hear him talk this way, but I proceeded to ask him about the time frame of his plan.

"A few years — it doesn't matter," he answered. "We can wait. We have inscrutable patience. That happens to be what those of Western culture fail to understand about us," he continued. "They look for quick solutions, like the TV dinners they pop into their ovens.

"But we know better. We have time on our side because we make time our friend. For them, for the Americans, for those enslaved by public opinion, time is the deadliest of enemies!"

I thought about his words again and again — *enslaved by public opinion.*

He was right, of course, as he so often was. When you are willing to sacrifice a hundred thousand fellow countrymen, or half a million, their opinion is of little consequence.

There is no dictatorship over the dead.

We seemed to be brothers in the faith, dedicated to the same goals. We wanted to bring our country up to a higher standard of living. We wanted to rid it of the last vestiges of any foreign influence. I was assigned the economic aspects of our plan.

Saad took over all else. That was when he served as minister of defense. The president was his brother-in-law.

The president died six months later.

I asked Saad about this.

He assured me he had nothing to do with it. "His physician said his heart just gave up," he said. A tragedy, he called it.

Saad became president within a week.

The next few years were quite wonderful. We built bridges, hospitals, power plants. School after school was constructed. Oil revenues were at their highest level. We held our heads high in the community of nations. And then the war with our neighbor nation began.

All these years later, it is impossible for me to remember who started it. At the outset I assumed it was the other government. Saad would never be so belligerent, I thought.

How could I have been so stupid?

Easily, I decided. I was stupid because he knew I would be. He was a master at getting people to believe in him.

And that was his power. Men would die for him. Women would give up their young sons to fight for any cause he extolled.

But eventually I saw what was wrong.

And it was the super-bunker that opened my eyes.

Perhaps it would be useful for those of you unfamiliar with the super-bunker to see this particular clipping before you continue.

—M.F

SAAD NASUR SAFE IN SUPER-BUNKER

From the Associated Press

HAMBURG, Germany — A German newspaper reports that Saad Nasur remains safe from U.S. air attacks in a nuclear-bomb-proof bunker built underneath his shattered presidential palace.

Storage chambers inside are presently "filled to the ceiling" with plentiful stocks of food and various kinds of medicine. Up to twenty-five people could hold out in the bunker for "more than a year without undue worry," the report in the Sunday newspaper said.

The bunker's walls, ceiling and foundation are a full six feet thick, built with special concrete for added strength. The doors are made of steel-reinforced concrete one foot thick, accessible only via German-built elevators. The bunker can reportedly withstand heat of up to 572 degrees Fahrenheit; thus a nuclear blast from above would produce only a slight vibration. Ducts and filters bring fresh air into the complex. Even the water used for flushing the toilets is specially processed so that chemical agents are prevented from entering the system.

The transcript from George Hawatmeh's tape recordings continues:

I had not known about this super-bunker until after the plans had already been drawn up. When I stumbled upon a set of these, I hastened to confront Saad with them.

He was in his office. I threw the papers down on his rosewood desk. He looked up, ready to snarl, but seeing that it was I, he stopped — I was the only one, it had seemed until then, who could get away with criticism; others who had thought he would not punish them were wrong, dead wrong.

He smiled crookedly. "I see that you know."

"Yes, I do, Saad," I answered. "Tell me this is a flight of fancy. Tell me it is going to be large enough to hold all our generals, our intellectuals, our most valuable citizens. And even then, though I might be somewhat relieved, I would still mourn for the millions lost on battlefields beyond the parameters of your safe domain!"

He looked up at me, cupped his hands together and clapped them in mock applause.

"Brilliant, George," he said sarcastically. "Best performance yet. *Much* better than that time you met with the British prime minister about our terrorist attack on the House of Commons; I thought then that you were only marginally convincing. But you were believed nevertheless. However, *now!* The right amount of passion, rage, conviction. *Bravo!*"

His cold words stung me like a slap in the face.

Then he leaned forward over the desk, his expression suddenly dark, serious, those eyes steady.

"Of course, you and I both know that killing people hasn't been any problem for you in the past," he said. "Sometimes you did it yourself, let me remind you; sometimes you arranged it by proxy, *hiring* men

for the task. There is blood on your
hands, and, I agree, on my own, George,"
he told me. "The question is, which of us
has enjoyed it more?"

Those words stayed with me through the
night, robbing me of any sleep whatsoever.

Which of us has enjoyed it more? I asked
myself time and again.

How could Saad have been correct? For
himself, yes, that was eminently believ-
able, but for me?

Later I knew that he was, in a perverse
but accurate way, quite correct in what he
had said. I did enjoy the killing. I sat
at my desk day in and day out, reading the
reports, the long lists of enemy casualties. I rejoiced.

And yet those in our neighbor nation
would have the very same reaction. Later,
with the Allies arrayed against us, it
would be no different.

During the "mother of all battles" can
any American, except those in the anti-war
movement, can any English person, any
French person, anyone who is Turkish or
Italian or Egyptian or any other national-
ity, can *any* of them deny a surge through
their bodies, a momentary high when they
hear or read of a hundred more, a thousand, yea, ten thousand more bodies fallen
on the battlefields of our tortured region? When rivers of oil are ignited and
human flesh runs from it, aflame? So long
as the dying, so long as the wounded, are
on the *other* side, then it is proper, then
it is *not* subhuman to let out a cry of

celebration, because it is enemy blood that stains the desert sands!

One side in tragedy over a loss that can never be repaired, the other in mockery of all that has happened.

I enjoyed the killing because every enemy soldier who died brought victory that much closer for *us*.

I look at myself in a dirty mirror, and I am now ashamed.

But there is more than my shame. There is the shame of a nation that allowed itself to be seduced by a monster whom they looked up to as a messiah.

Saad Nasur, once a friend, now a monster

But then this is not new. All loyalty is as the shifting sand dunes in my part of the world, this place of Decameron. And I am the chief offender.

Saad had not let me know about the bunker because he knew I would object. He knew I would object to his willingness to let our countrymen meet their doom while he lived in relative comfort underground. For him there would be air-conditioning, food, water, whatever else he needed, *all waiting for him even now*.

I went to bed that night, and I slept, yes, if you can call what I endured sleep. My poor wife complained that I tossed and turned every few minutes.

It is no wonder.

My nightmare involved the bunker.

It was nearly a year after Saad had gone inside. All around him our beloved country had been devastated, but not just by the wartime acts of the international coalition. Finally it was by Saad himself.

He had planted bombs containing chemical and biological warheads at the remaining military sites, set to massive timers which he would trigger as soon as he was safely in the bunker.

He could not endure the Allies' reaping any of his sophisticated equipment, and there was no time to destroy each weapon, each advanced computer, each highly regarded weapon, on an individual basis.

He saw a major dividend in what would happen. He was thinking:

My people will experience the havoc, and they will blame it all on the Allies. There will be newscasts worldwide showing the devastation that results. The Muslim community will rise up in outrage. Our deluded brothers in the coalition will revolt and turn against the oppressors. And I shall emerge as leader of all, savior of Islam.

And so it went.

But that was not the totality of this nightmare.

Inside the huge structure Saad was joking, laughing, eating, drinking, whoring with captive women.

Outside, Al-Khari seemed like a fairy tale for infants in comparison to the legions of children wandering along bombed-out avenues, picking their way through rubble, crying, their bodies riddled with disease.

There are others in the ravaged landscape, women whose clothes have become tat-
tered rags, their nakedness a display of
burns and sores. Men, too, of course, men
with armless torsos, with no hands to ex-
tend in supplication if anyone remained
who could help.

Oh, yes. The nightmare will soon have
ended, in that darkness, at least. But —
the idea terrified me — what about when I
awaken?

Nearly a year has passed in my dream.

My nightmare has gone forward in time,
like tape in a video player.

Flash ahead.

Let us see what happens. We can hardly
wait.

Saad and the others emerge, confident
that he will be victorious. He stands,
shocked, at what awaits him. An army, yes,
but not of the coalition. An army of his
own people. They have been waiting there
for the rat to pop up from his sewer. In
shifts. Twenty-four hours a day.

He finally emerges.

They raise their rifles. They aim.

"I did it for you," he screams. "I have
a vision for this nation."

He howls in pain, turns.

A woman, a bloody knife in her hand,
screams, "You!"

She smiles sadly as she plunges the
weapon into his chest and he falls back-
ward, covered with liquid red.

The gathered multitude shouts in exulta-
tion.

DARK KNIGHT

The woman turns the knife on herself as she cries, *"I can no longer live without my beloved!"*

My wife, my widow.

Nightmares come and go. But the images from this one lingered long after the morning sun arose.

I wondered, oh, how I wondered what that nightmare was supposed to be telling me.

And then I knew.

I am not in that bunker. He has closed the heavy door behind him — and in my face.

I am left to die with the others.

And this I do.

I awoke, yes, the night behind me, my weary body covered with the clinging sweat of my fear, and from that time on, each moment of every passing day, I have been driven to ask, What does real life have in store for me?

The answer to George Hawatmeh's question came quickly enough — within a few weeks in fact.

He was arrested and tortured.

Directly in charge of this was Saad Nasur himself, not an underling; no, no, he could not let it be *that*.

Saad Nasur personally applied electrodes to George Hawatmeh's body.

Saad Nasur flicked the switch that turned on the current, first with just a little voltage, giving his former friend a taste of pain.

Saad Nasur turned the dial that increased the dosage, stretching this out as long as possible to maximize the anguish.

Nor did he stop when George Hawatmeh was dead.

He stalked over to the body, took a Persian hunting knife, the kind with a serrated blade, and cut open George Hawatmeh's throat.

"I wanted no chance that he happened to be in a coma, and therefore his body somehow could be faking death," he reportedly told an aide, who later defected to Allied forces.

The aide went on to say that the blood on Saad Nasur's hands was not washed off for at least an hour after the act.

The reason?

"He felt a sense of reassurance from holding up those hands and looking at them every few minutes," the aide replied. "Reassurance that the blood of life was no longer coursing through George Hawatmeh's veins."

This man's wife and three sons were arrested shortly after his death.

They were forced to eat uncooked pieces of his flesh and then they were beheaded, one by one, the survivors having to watch in terror and disgust as the grisly ceremony proceeded in each case.

Finally all five bodies were cremated and mixed together in a common ivory urn, which Saad Nasur kept as a paperweight on his presidential desk.

That same day a generous Saad Nasur gave a brand-new Chevrolet Nomad to each of his 150 field commanders.

M_ouphas Fakarian...._

Instances of Saad's generosity are hardly scarce. But one has to realize that such as these are premeditated, with not the slightest degree of genuine charity motivating anything he does.

A master of manipulation? Truly so. A supreme genius at manipulating the emotions of those around him, a corrupt puppet-master from whom few had extricated themselves.

To him the gift of food is just a bribe. There is no humanitarian dimension to this man, none whatsoever.

And yet it was not always so with Saad Nasur.

There was a time....

Saad Nasur, at one point, was a university student in the United States.

In those days that was considered an ultimate achievement for a young man from our country.

It is said that the parting for his journey was emotional, deeply so. One of his brothers told me about the day he and his mother, his father and his two other brothers went with Saad to the dusty old air terminal.

"You can make it," his mother had told him. "Do it, Saad — do it for all of us; not just for this family but for the whole nation."

He boarded the plane, then turned and waved to them.

They were all he had in life.

His parents convinced him he would make nothing of himself if he didn't get away from the influences in our homeland, influences that were deteriorating annually, with no improvement in sight — the governmental corruption, the feeling of hopelessness among the people.

They thought the United States would give him new hope, the right kind of education, the tools for a better life. In their village — or anywhere else, for that matter — his friends were only friends so long as he was able to do favors for them. If any of them could get more food, more money, more sex by somehow betraying Saad Nasur, none would hesitate to do so.

Only his family remained loyal.

Only they could be depended upon.

Perhaps in the United States it would be different.

Perhaps he could find the kindness, the decency, the honor for which his soul longed.

Saad was a foreign exchange student at the spacious Westwood campus of UCLA. One of the students in his dorm recalled meeting Saad Nasur as a young college student.

This excerpt is from a Los Angeles newspaper article which appeared shortly after the invasion.

"He seemed like a pretty nice guy when we first met," remembers local attorney Range Johnson. "I remember he had a hard time understanding American humor, but he was pretty sharp. I couldn't understand his humor either, so I guess that made us even. He said he liked Americans because we were so friendly. I thought he was a pretty decent guy back then."

According to Johnson, the two went to see a film about black drug dealers that evening. But when they arrived at the theater, a group of young blacks began to go berserk. Apparently they had been told that the showing they wanted to attend was sold out.

One of the youths accused the manager of not wanting to let in "niggers."

Although the manager insisted that more than half the audience already inside was black, Johnson said the youth slipped on a pair of brass knuckles and hit the manager, breaking his jaw. A riot broke out, and the police showed up soon afterward.

" 'Welcome to America!' I told him," said Johnson.

"We decided not to stick around, so we worked our way through the crowd to leave," he said. "But by then a police barricade had been erected at each of the streets leading into the neighborhood.

"Saad was beginning to panic, and he kept asking, 'What do we do?' "

"I told him just to stay calm. 'If you don't act suspicious,' I said, 'they won't do anything to you.' I was wrong."

According to Johnson, both of them were dragged by several policemen to a nearby police van.

"I tried to tell the officers that we hadn't done anything," Johnson said, "but they just told me to shut up. One of them told me if I opened my mouth again, he was going to break my jaw. It was then that Saad Nasur punched the policeman, breaking *his* jaw. Then the others started beating on Saad with their nightsticks. I kept screaming that they were going to kill him, but they just threw me in the back of the police van and drove off. I could still see a group of them beating on him as we left."

Johnson said he didn't see Saad Nasur again until the following week. In the meantime Johnson was released on bail and proceeded to file suit against the city for violation of his civil rights.

"I couldn't believe it when they dropped the case," Johnson said. "It seems my newfound buddy had told the police and the investigators that I was lying, that I was resisting arrest and trying to attack the cops. I knew then that somebody had gotten to him. At the time I didn't know if they had threatened to deport him or what. Later I found out that a little bribery was all it took for him to betray a friend."

According to Johnson, a black hospital orderly confessed that the local police chief had arranged for better hospital treatment for Saad Nasur and dropped the charges against him for breaking the policeman's jaw in ex-

change for his denial of the alleged incident.

"When I asked the orderly how he could have been involved in such a cover-up against another brother, he just said, 'We survive any way we can,'" Johnson said.

"Saad Nasur had moved into this fancy apartment off-campus, and I went over to confront him with what I had found out," Johnson said. "He didn't even deny it. 'I do what I must,' he told me with this cold expression on his face. I told him I had thought we were buddies, but he pointed out that we had known each other for only one day when the incident occurred. We argued, and I left the apartment. Outside, some policemen had just pulled up. They grabbed me and started beating me right there on the lawn in front of the apartment building. Saad was just standing there in the doorway of his apartment, watching. I've always suspected he was the one who called the police in the first place," Johnson added.

Today, Johnson, a civil rights lawyer, is blind in one eye and still walks with a heavy limp from injuries allegedly sustained in that incident. Within a week of the beating, Johnson says, public outcry forced the resignation of the city's chief of police. And that was the last time he ever saw Saad Nasur.

I believe that was part of the process of corrupting of Saad Nasur. But there were other incidents as well.

Saad Nasur did not switch from what he was to what he became in the course of a few days.

According to the entries in his private diaries from those early days, it took longer, a great deal longer, to reach the soul of this man — for the increasingly corrosive forces within American society to eat away anything that happened to be good, the residue of any moral consciousness that might have remained from the mother country.

These came at him from a variety of directions.

He saw the racism.

He saw the "selling" of religion via television hucksters, each program full of bright lights and loud music and smiling faces, and plenty of pitches for donations, making him think that Islam, more than ever, was the true religion and that Christianity was a charade.

(I know better, of course, but more about that later; more about that searing change in my own life, that clear redefinition of one Mouphas Fakarian as a human being.)

He learned of the manipulation of stocks and bonds by men who had only the acquisition of more wealth at the center of their value systems, regardless of the harm caused to other investors.

And then there was the nightly televised violence of the gang-infested streets of Los Angeles and Miami and elsewhere.

"It is safer in my country to walk the streets at midnight than in any big American city!" one of his entries read.

He began to wonder what the United States had to offer him. Certainly not its superficial, glitzy religion. Nor the dubious integrity of its financial dealings. Nor any politi-.cal —

"Then why am I here?" he wrote.

He had no answer, nothing good and reasonable and fulfilling.

So he decided to return. But he had little money. That was when he found out how useful drug dealing was.

He made money doing that. And he learned about terror, the use of intimidation to get what he wanted.

He took all that back to the mother country with him.

He left for America to get an education.

And he succeeded.

$\mathbf{A}$s the publisher of this forthcoming book, I sit back quietly for a moment now and catch my breath.

And I wonder.

I wonder about how much evil, how much pain, how much crime could have been prevented if the "authorities" had conducted themselves in a different manner — not according to their own inbred biases but rather as they should have been doing from the beginning, protecting and serving the public.

In Los Angeles, I am told, the police cars have a motto painted on each side:

TO PROTECT AND TO SERVE

But that was conveniently forgotten as, according to the numerous newspaper and television reports, they beat a young black man nearly to death, clubbing him, kicking him, while others stood by and watched.

It would have been the same if the victim had been Hispanic. Being black or Hispanic in Los Angeles can mean living life under a death sentence.

But there is more to it than that, for there have been other beatings in other towns, in other cities, by other police officers.

Why now? Why so many so suddenly?

Mouphas stumbled upon the answer. Here is one piece of it....

Suppressed column from German news magazine—presented here intact. The editorial staff resigned after this was squelched and decided to spread word via the international media about what had happened. This column stirred up some significant responses, as you shall see from the material following it.

—M.F

THE MAD PATH

Have we not learned?

Have we so buried the past that we have forgotten its lessons altogether?

Or when these can no longer be suppressed by our inherent psychological defense mechanisms, do we choose simply not to face up to them but try however we might to ignore their very existence and continue along this mad path of our conscienceless repetition?

It was as a nation that we embarked on that same odyssey in the 1930s, calling it national pride and other patriotic words as a cloak of deception, a façade behind which were the rabid mutterings of the men — dare we dignify them as such? — we had chosen to lead us.

After World War II, when the fatherland was ashambles, we said for the world to hear, *no more, no more, no more.*

We were believed.

We were believed enough for the world to trust us as our divided country became one again decades later when the German chancellor faced the community of nations and proclaimed, "We have learned our lesson. We have reformed.

We will never again be responsible for the slaughter of Jews."

What a lie! The worst kind. A lie that no one dares imagine is anything but the truth.

...*we will never again be responsible for the slaughter of Jews.*

But we are. We are indeed.

The gas.

The germs.

Azazi missiles dropped them on Tel Aviv and Riyahd.

The strategy was so simple: Engage in "regular" attacks for several weeks and thereby lull the Jews and the turncoat Arabs into thinking that Saad Nasur did, after all, lack the nerve to bring Israel into the war, which using gas and germs surely would provoke. That was why only conventional warheads were used the first time, the twentieth time.

And then came the gas, the germs.

The Patriot missiles shoot the Azazis down, with debris spread over a wide area, along with the gas, the germs. Most of the odorless gas dissipates; most of the invisible germs die in midair. But some get through, and also during the next attack, and the attack after that.

All the same night.

We have done it again.

We have succeeded in trapping some Jews, not on the scale of the Third Reich, but sufficient for the moment. We have wiped out men, women and children.

But this time it is different. This time it is by proxy. *Our* hands are not dirty. Look, see for yourself!

Collective institutional deception.

An interesting press release was issued from Berlin when suspicions were beginning to leak out:

"Certain German companies have violated the internal embargo by selling nonmilitary medical goods only. Any other sales occurred before the embargo went into effect. Be assured that we will continue to monitor this situation quite carefully."

Where was the shame

evidenced over those "other sales before the embargo went into effect"?

It was all so neat, so detached. Fellow Germans, we have done what we have done, and that is it.

Yet that was not to be it at all.

We received a FAX message from a clinic in Tel Aviv. It detailed the deaths of a dozen very young children from an orphanage near that port city. They died both from nerve gas *and* germs released by the intruding SCUDs. There was a vague mention from enemy sources about retaliation for the massacre at Al-Khari and the implication that many more canisters of various poisons and disease were at the disposal of Saad Nasur.

So many of those helpless ones were literally eaten away, from their insides out, and at the same time they were made to endure the most horrendous epileptic-like seizures.

Veteran surgeons became weak when they operated on any children who managed to last longer than their comrades, opening up their stomachs to find colonies of germs thriving.

"It was like stumbling upon some sort of grotesque beehive each time," observed one surgeon.

There were other incidents comparable to these, layers of the true face of Islam peeled up one after the other, including the shameful treatment of POWs, which tended to enrage other governments to the extent that even certain Muslim leaders condemned that treatment as "undignified."

At that time this did not seem a particularly severe denunciation until non-Muslims realized that so-called dignity was a pillar of the Islamic code of conduct — at least for those of the faith who were devout though non-political, that group which urged restraint on the more anti-Western militants, telling them that the world would judge Islam by the example of their ill-conceived actions.

Indeed the world did judge!

The Muslims were to be condemned in subsequent days, heathens acting according to uncivilized and the most perverse impulses.

Men riding camels in a desert land, these ignorant men thumbing their noses at the rest of the world!

While elsewhere sane people and their sane governments recoiled in horror at the barbarity of it all.

There was the unholy brilliance of the scheme.

Scheme, we say?

Yes, we say that. We say it, and we mean it. An intricate scheme dreamed up by a few powerful men in a few influential companies, men still dedicated to the ideals of the figure they continue to idolize: Adolf Hitler.

They sell to Saad Nasur all the chemicals he could possibly want. They sell to him all the antibiotics. They add his billions to the respective bottom lines of their cash-rich companies.

They send over advisers to counsel the likes of Saad Nasur, these stupid little errand boys carrying with them sheets of paper with complex formulas scrawled on both sides, calling the contents of the sealed envelopes they carry mere friendly letters of greeting from some admirers of his living in the heart of German industrial might, those same businessmen whose craven parents aided the great and glorious führer.

We have not changed, you see. We have gone from public infamy to private infamy, from an infamy well-chronicled for more than half a century to an infamy kept secret for far fewer years.

We have done it again. We Germans have known that we have done it. And we have done *nothing* to stop any of it. We have looked the other way — oh, how good we are at that — *not* at the guilt that washes like a tidal wave over us. We have done this because of what one ex-Bundestag politician has rightly called greed.

But, of course, that

was only part of the truth.

Greed was not the principal catalyst behind this uncustomary column that you are now reading, for it must be acknowledged that, sadly, greed is no longer newsworthy in human affairs.

Ah, you see, there are a multitude of dark and unholy acts in this our world of which mankind by itself is incapable, their commission requiring a partner to join with some unwary human, even to *enter* and possess that individual, and in the course of doing so, shredding any remaining decency, any fragments of conscience still clinging tenuously to the Dark Knight and others in his inner circle, ultimately leaving goodness and mercy and decency among the gray, cold ashes of their spent and melancholy land of Eden.

Could it be accurate? Could journalists be maintaining any token shred of their professional integrity by suggesting that, once, it was so that Saad Nasur was less evil, less terrifying?

That might be so. That might be so.

Years ago he was considered the friend of hundreds of Jews, Jews he had helped when he discovered that they were starving in some isolated corner of his country. He sent them food. He had doctors treat their illnesses. He gave them money. Thus there is today a small handful left, Jews who have nothing but a good picture in their minds of this tyrant, from a time when that may not have been so.

Under normal circumstances we as journalists would not be writing in this manner, but nothing of what besets us here in the German fatherland and beyond is normal. In fact, the extent of the egomaniacal impulses of Saad Nasur fails psychiatric dissection altogether.

But then what could be said of him can be said in large measure of vast segments of our people, of a near-totality of those who call themselves German, of this proud and vibrant community of our countrymen.

One writer, the noted William L. Shirer, expressed it best in his book *A Native's Return* (Little, Brown and Company), an unofficial sequel to *The Rise and Fall of the Third Reich*:

"After the Nazi years I no longer felt any affinity for the Germans. A people who could behave so bestially, who could treat others with so much brutality, who could try to massacre a whole people because of their race, who had such a lust for domination, who so savagely violated the human spirit, were they not barbarians who had to be watched and restrained? How could you trust them not to break out again, as they had under Bismarck, Wilhelm II and then Hitler? Philosophers and statesmen and historians said you could not condemn an entire people. But this entire people, with a few honorable exceptions, had joined together under the primitive swastika to participate in unspeakable crimes. They were not to be condemned for it? They were not to be held responsible? They were to be trusted?"

We Germans, now united after so long, can no longer be proud of what has befallen our nation. Nor can we be content to sit and do nothing while the evil mentality that once generated such havoc again begins its slow march, awakening from a slumber forced upon it by the champions of those it victimized half a century earlier.

We have no wolves howling at our gates just now, no bony beggar hands banging loudly for entrance to our meager storehouses, for we are presently quite fat as a nation, fat from the plentiful harvest that has been our destiny for so long now.

But deranged men *inside* this our house, attempting to satiate their unholy obsessions — yes, *that* is another story!

— The Editorial Staff

M*ouphas Fakarian back....*

In other words, the German mentality hasn't reformed. It has learned only one lesson from the past: When you are engaged in what might be called "certain activities," do it as secretly as possible.

Keep everything under cover.

Don't jump to the war option so quickly and spectacularly.

Keep a façade of respectability.

And if you are somehow caught doing what you are doing, be sure and profess, immediately, official ignorance, coupled with a promise of an intensive investigation at the highest levels of government.

Shout the accusation of anti-German bigotry from the rooftops if there are any in the media and elsewhere who just don't believe you. They don't like to be tarred with that one! You'll defuse the crisis in no time.

As could be imagined, the circulation of that banned column created an enormous uproar in the world press, especially among the American television news commentators. But there was curiously little issuing from the American White House about the developments.

Why did the magazine's publisher try to keep the contents from ever being circulated?

Journalists did not have to dig very far to find out why.

The controlling stockholder was the CEO of a company with a unique history.

The CEO's father was president of a German chemicals firm that supplied the concentration camps with whatever was needed in terms of gases, germ cultures and proper training with all such.

After the war the father was questioned about this.

His response was simply, "It was all a business transaction, you must understand. We manufactured; they bought. As simple as that."

"But what about the *use* to which those materials were being put?" a reporter asked.

"I couldn't control that," the president of that company replied.

"Would you have refused to go through any such sales if you could have done so?" the reporter persisted.

"I have to go now," the man stated, and hurried from the room.

This time his son is in charge. And this time, as CEO, when the son was asked a similar question, he responded by hurrying from quite another room. The principle was, of course, the same.

But his behavior was guaranteed to whet the appetites of

journalists whose thirst for juicy news often could be deplored; in this case, however, they deserved applause for what they uncovered.

Anti-Semitism has never died throughout the German industrial community. It was not buried in the rubble strewn across Germany after World War II. It was only intensified. Jews were blamed along with the Allies.

Hatred of Jews lives and breathes as vibrantly today as it did half a century ago. It is rooted in the German culture, in the German obsession for excellence and dominance. To the German mind, excellence is simply a code word for purity — the purity of the Aryan race.

When there were opportunities to sell his company's products to yet another devil, whatever the ghastly consequences, the CEO had no compunctions. After all, his father had done so. And the son had been raised to carry on in adherence to the same business ethic.

He began to feel invincible in direct correlation to the growth of Germany as the dominant power on the European continent, and especially when the two Germanies united.

"No one will be able to touch us now," he once bragged to a friend. "We can bring back the glory days of the past."

An alliance with Saad Nasur was part of the heinous plan this industrialist had in mind.

He would benefit in three intertwined ways: (1) His company would earn many billions; (2) he would cultivate a friend in Saad Nasur, and word had it that Saad never forgot *loyal* friends; (3) he would open the door to a massacre of the Zionists, which in turn would force Israel to retaliate, and that would unite the entire Arab world against the Allies.

When I, Mouphas Fakarian, found out bits and pieces of the foregoing, I scoffed. Surely it was part of a disinformation campaign by the Zionists themselves.

And yet later the truth did assemble everything in a whole that was unimpeachable.

I ask you these questions:

Why were there no German troops in the coalition?

Why was only a token amount of money pledged by Bonn to offset the mushrooming costs of the operation? The Japanese paid several hundred percent more than Germany did.

It could be said that the constitutions of both countries prevented any such military participation.

Is that reasonable? Is that just?

Yet the German constitution apparently *permitted* the war effort *against* the Allies' enemy, however deviously this was arranged. Is this what the chancellor and others would dupe us into believing?

Nevertheless, the Japanese were enthusiastic supporters of the war effort. And they put their billions behind their words.

The Germans? Anemic with their verbal and political support. And anemic as well with their financial support.

The reason is clear enough: If they went too far in favor of the Allies, Saad Nasur was going to release the most damaging evidence about the Bonn government's clandestine support of his regime.

That is a scandal worthy of the name.

scandal?

Oh, yes, it was indeed a scandal. But, by far, I tell you, it was not the only one — no, it was not.

Let me pose another question: It is one thing to point a justifiably accusing finger at Bonn. It is one thing to hint of Nazi influence in the German government of today and in industry, strange little men who would like nothing better than to add a few hundred, a few thousand, a few hundred thousand Jews to the total tallied up during the glory days of World War II.

But then — and here is the question — what about the *American* companies that also, directly or indirectly, participated in the militarization of my country, thereby strengthening the hand of Saad Nasur?

That Silicon Valley electronic outfit? The aircraft firm or the pharmaceutical company?

All grabbed a piece of the pie that Saad Nasur offered as bait.

But no one guessed what sort of leader he was in *those* days, you might protest. No one can be condemned for what hindsight reveals.

Not so.

The espionage intelligence community knew in astonishing detail what Saad Nasur was like.

No illusions existed among *them*, nor were there any illusions at the Pentagon.

He was evil.

But Saad Nasur was an evil man who seemed to be a dependable ally of the United States.

After all, that was the important consideration, was it not?

And wasn't that why the United States supported him against our neighbor in a long war between the two countries?

Why was the history of the Land of the Free so replete with relationships with men such as Noriega, Marcos and so many others?

Whatever the reasoning, American companies chose to deal with the devil, chose to sell their souls along with their commodities, as it were.

Yet we must get beyond the companies themselves. As in Germany, there was supposed to be competent *regulation* of this sort of thing, in place wholly to eliminate the kinds of abuses that do creep into any free-trade society. And that regulation rested in the dirty hands of materialistic legislators who were supposed to be looking out for the interests of American citizens — which is why they were elected in the first place — and yet, in the final analysis, who were quite easily bribed to put aside any scruples they might have had and look the other way.

Bribed?

Isn't that a dangerous word to be bruiting about? Yes, it is, but it applies here. It describes just what went on in the corridors of Congress and in back rooms and other places in Washington, D.C.

Saad Nasur bribed corporate officials. And corporate officials bribed senators and other influentials in government.

There is one senator in particular who fills me with the most noxious loathing.

He stood up early against any Allied attack. He proclaimed shame over what *his* government was contemplating, over the potential of horrendous numbers of American casualties, and he raised the spectre of another Vietnam.

Clever, this man.

While he was issuing forth with such noble words, his left hand pounding the podium, his right hand was reaching out behind him and accepting tainted money from, shall we say, certain interests with various contacts in the Middle East!

But Saad Nasur did not stop there, not with members of the American Congress nor of the business community.

He even bought out the entire anti-war movement.

Which is not to say that everyone in the movement was on his payroll, for by no means is that true.

But certainly the organizers were. Clever men, yes, clever in how successful they were in getting others to follow them in a mindless and stupid fashion, like sheep bleating noisily along the way.

Fortunately, this time the American public as a whole did not get sucked into this latest game of chess perpetrated by a foreign power to weaken the resolve to win the war at hand.

Most Americans saw the anti-war protesters for what they really were, deluded simpletons who had no conception of what they were really doing. Ask the average one to explain or defend his or her views, and all you heard was inarticulate double-talk, a kind of nonsensical party line.

But it was not for lack of trying, as the expression goes. Saad did his very best.

And one of his first lackeys was a pitiable individual who generated the greatest possible sympathy — a certain high-profile Vietnam vet. This one had lost his arms and legs in that war, and so it seemed impossible to hate someone who had suffered so much.

Which raises yet another question: At what point did he cross from honest indignation over a new war to exploiting his physical condition for purely self-centered and even treasonous motives?

And at what point do we pull back from basic human sympathy to a rational view of just what an individual is trying to accomplish?

Hidden agendas.

Yes, always among *this* crowd, this crowd of so-called anti-war patriots. That isn't necessarily a contradiction in terms, not by any means, but the *way* these anti-everything people wrap an emasculated form of patriotism around themselves to hide their hidden agendas!

So many of them carry their placards and walk safely up and down their cute little Main Streets, dripping with Americana, and expect the rest of the population to fall for this sort of manipulation.

Not this time.

And that chap in the wheelchair.

He is among the worst offenders, a deeply bitter man with darkly paranoid views and surrounded by a group of friends from a faction of American politics that is shameful at best.

All my doubts about this man will dissipate the day a full discovery is made of his Byzantine connections with Saad Nasur. And any other anti-American monster who happens along.

Little of the sort has come to light as yet.

I pray that I am alive when it happens. I so want to see

the reaction of the public to the truth, the *real* truth, not the biased, jaundiced "truth" they have been spoon-fed from so many in the media.

But there is more. One man in a wheelchair doesn't amount to much of a revolution.

The "more" of which I write, *that* will also shock you, my readers. You may be inclined, after reading what I write next, to throw my book aside as just so much paranoia.

Please don't.

Please don't.

How long has it been that we have known each other, Mouphas?

I can see, as I look back, how much you have changed over the years, from being a Muslim party-liner to being a Christian. You outlasted Mokahr, your teacher.

The torture that man underwent! Not because of his Christianity. Saad had known about that all along. Mokahr was the only non-Muslim in his cabinet. The torture was inflicted because Mokahr had been planning to overthrow him and had gotten several of the generals to support a coup attempt.

As often was the case, Saad had the gift of timing, and he acted quickly. The generals were shot in the head. But Mokahr — he would be dealt with in a very special way. As George Hawatmeh had been.

But your friend didn't betray you, Mouphas.

You never found out who did.

M_ouphas Fakarian here...._

On the West Coast of the United States, the East Coast, in the Midwest, elsewhere.

Brutality.

By police officers. Against near-helpless men. Dozens of cases coming to light.

Today. Now.

Why?

There are reasons, the most terrifying of reasons, and there are people behind those reasons.

The industrialists.

The madmen from the Rhineland _together with a secret_

Islamic paragovernmental group set up by Saad Nasur for the purpose of destabilizing the United States.

The target: police departments from California to Maine.

These are being infiltrated to an increasing degree by closet neo-Nazis and card-carrying Ba'ath Party members — and they are really one and the same, you know — hate-possessed men who all start out behind the false front of being respectable members of the department.

They are content to await the right moment.

Saad Nasur and the cash-rich executive vice presidents of several German companies formulated the plan together a decade earlier, and it is only now being activated, because the climate is at last right, in their view.

It cannot be said that all cases of brutality against blacks or Latinos have stemmed from this plan. But all have been applauded.

The father of the neo-Nazi movement in the United States was quoted as saying that "my people are everywhere. We *are*, you know. In government. In industry. In police departments all over this nation. You can't stop us. If you try, blood will run like rivers in the towns and the cities of America."

Terrifying? Yes, it is.

And yet, as I have said, this and other portions of the book in which I have invested my life may cause some readers to be so skeptical that they turn their backs on the truth, saying it cannot be so, and what a poor chap this Mouphas Fakarian is, deserving only pity, if not contempt.

As a result of the ghastly acts of a few saboteurs, and they *are* saboteurs of a sort, the men and women not involved in this plan of Saad Nasur's, and who have been sworn to uphold the law, could come to be seen by the public as the enemies, as the true outlaws. And that will open the door for so-called housecleaning at departments around the nation, with more and more secret Nazis moving in to replace them.

That is happening now.

It must not be allowed to continue.

Most of the policemen in the United States are totally honest. Yet they will be increasingly suspect by virtue of the relative handful who owe their allegiance to a philosophy that is demonic at its very core.

Islam.

Far more frightening than communism. Because there are many more Muslims in the world than there are communists, especially now. The communists have never professed any role for God in their scheme of things. But the Muslims believe they are doing Allah's bidding. And the Germans will use anyone they can, directly or indirectly, to satiate the blood lust that has driven them on for most of this century.

Are these the end times?

I do not know that. I am not a theologian.

But I do know something else.

If not the end times, then never, never the best of times. Evil is afoot in the land, evil conducting its affairs in the shadow of the primitive swastika, as William Shirer wrote.

Satan has grown wiser over the years.

He has never been a stupid foe. But as his eternal judgment approaches, desperation has been the mother of invention for him. He does not need the blatant, practicing satanists as such. They have their place — indeed they do. Nor does he need the witches either. And one can discount the mass murderers as well.

All seem a little too obvious. But they do help to spread fear. They help to distract the public attention away from the really formidable foes — people you should be able to trust.

Senators. Police officers. And others.

Most are honest. Most find corruption and racism abhorrent.

But some revel in it.

They can last a long time. They have no money worries. At their disposal is an open line of credit. From Frankfurt and Dusseldorf and Bonn and other cities where the spirit of anti-Semitism merely slumbered for a while. From the Middle East, as men from my country and from others in that region gather together in secluded places and plan, licking their lips as they strategize, as they wait for the day when they will do the only thing that matters, the only reason any of them have for living.

To take over.

You see, nothing else matters to them.

Nothing.

Mouphas Fakarian continuing....

Quite frankly I was ready to close this strange and terrifying little volume, to end it at last with an earnest exhortation to be strong, to kneel before our holy Father God and to offer Him, as the supreme Creator, our most humble, frightened, expectant prayers through His risen and ascended Son, in the Person of the Holy Spirit.

Indeed, I was set to do all this when something within this frail frame of my being caused me to hesitate. It may be called a still, small voice perhaps, not voices, of course, *never* words. Some of those who say they hear *voices* I worry much about, for they tend to claim that whatever revelation

95

they get in this manner is, in and of itself, a direct communication from the Lord. Then they go on their way in obedience to that source which they do not know or even comprehend, and they blame it all on the Holy Spirit; for truly the third Person of the Trinity has had more blame laid at His feet than many of history's most condemned villains.

They blame it all on Him, whereas the directive or what was assumed to be a directive from heaven was nothing other than human subconscious flotsam rising to the surface, that dark and deep part of the mind filled with any manner of "wreckage."

How awful it is, how awful it will go on being, like an aging film star who shrinks from the bright lights until she had applied layers of makeup in the process of ever-so-fragile make-believe, hiding the pale and mocking old shell that she has become, struggling up from the pit of her debauchery and hoping that nobody notices...until the end times roar in like a lion of doom for untold millions, sweeping away all the selfish and petty and blasphemous games being played even within the body of Christ, or more particularly, particularly there, including the unholy and dishonoring tendency to which so many succumb.

As full members of the world-wide community of mankind, they have this unreasoning and unreasonable tendency to *use* their relationship, and a relationship often questionable at best, with the Creator in a way that *accommodates* them, regardless of scriptural validity, that plays to the satiation of their desires, however unbecoming these are, and not so much Him, not so much Almighty God, though He is retained in their connivings, maintaining the form if hardly the substance, despite any intention they might have.

Did I say intention? Yes, I did, but meaning pretension, meaning every letter of that word, maintaining the form if hardly the substance, and dragging·the seduced along with them to the lake of fire by way of the Great White Seat of Holy and Eternal Judgment.

As I said, I was ready to end this volume when I sat back in my chair for a moment and idly turned the knob on the radio in front of me.

I was about to turn the radio off and pack the remainder of my belongings when the announcement came through:

SAAD NASUR IS DEAD

There was dancing everywhere. Among non-Muslims, that is. As well as those of Islam who were called traitors by the rest.

Piece by piece, the story came through about what had happened. Even those who had publicly professed support for Saad Nasur sent their rejoicing to the community of nations.

But it was especially interesting, as everyone knows, *how* he died. Not as in the dream of George Hawatmeh. Not that at all.

Far differently....

Saad Nasur, the supreme ruler, was in isolation, having abandoned his bunker as untenable in the final analysis. Ba'athist sympathizers gave him refuge. There was a round-the-clock guard.

Saad Nasur had few visitors.

Nubal came, of course, to plot revenge. There were reports that they drew up a list of terrorist targets in the United States and England. A prime one was Grand Central Station.

"Brilliant!" Saad remarked, clapping his hands together. "You cause maximum pain with limited expenditure."

"It wasn't my idea," Nubal remarked more than a little cynically. "I picked it up from '60 Minutes.' "

"Of course!" Saad replied with appreciation. "The American media have been most helpful, haven't they?"

"Most helpful. I don't know where we'd be without them."

"Nuclear power plants as well?"

"Yes."

"And military bases?"

"Tougher, as you know, but hardly impossible, what with all that is presently available to us."

Nubal winked at Saad, and Saad knew exactly what he meant. They had so many contacts with defense contractors that getting the right passes to the right bases was simple.

"Through surrogates, we now *own* a small firm producing metal sheeting for one of their missiles," Nubal commented.

"That has happened since — ?" Saad started to ask but was interrupted by a hesitant guard who was signaling him over the intercom in the room where he and Nubal were meeting.

He paused, listening.

"All right, show her in," he said impatiently. "Tell her I have only thirty seconds."

Nubal had heard.

"They still idolize you," he said.

"And so it will be when we ultimately triumph, you and I," Saad replied.

The guard at the door to that room knocked.

"Enter," Saad shouted.

"Is it convenient now, sir?" the guard asked.

"I have already said so. Show her in."

An elderly woman came into the room, her deeply lined face smiling as she glimpsed Saad.

"O Great One," she said, quickly falling to her knees in front of him.

"You have a gift for me?" he inquired with strained patience.

"I do, I do," she replied. "This humble footwear, woven by my own hand, master."

She held out a small box.

Nubal reacted immediately and started to grab it from her.

"Don't be such an alarmist," Saad rebuked him. "My guards have already checked, remember?"

"One cannot be too careful," Nubal said, offended that he had been spoken to in that manner in front of a common peasant.

Saad touched the crown of the old woman's head in a beneficent gesture and then sent her on her way.

He opened the little box carefully, despite his protestation about the meticulous quality of the protection his loyal guards had shown then and always.

A pair of wool socks.

Saad looked at them admiringly.

"Very nice," he said. "Such a simple gift."

"Of love, of devotion," Nubal added. "Remember that, please, if you should ever become discouraged over what the *people* think of you. Forget the stupid *governments*, Saad."

Deeply moved, Saad replaced the lid of the box and put it aside, while he and Nubal conversed well into the night, fortified by occasional shots of bourbon. Finally, they could no longer keep their eyes open and bid one another good-bye until breakfast that morning.

He slept until 10:30. His wife and the children had arisen an hour before and were waiting for him.

But he hadn't been awakened.

No one dared to do that except in wartime or a political emergency.

It was to be a special working breakfast, with Nubal, with commanders of their underground units in Italy, France, Germany, England. Only in Germany did they have an easy time of it. There was a crackdown in all the other countries, especially in England, where that woman's successor was proving to be every bit as dangerous as she had been — perhaps more so, it seemed.

But the most important aspect was the presence of the one who had flown in from the United States.

The founder of Aryans Against Racial Pollution.

AARP liked the irony of having the same initials as a highly respected organization established to protect the rights of elderly Americans. Anything that led to confusion in the minds of the public aided the cause embraced by Saad Nasur and others of his ilk.

This individual had brought his handsome, blond-haired son with him.

"AARP's new image," he had declared proudly the day before as he introduced the lad.

They all were waiting for Saad.

After bathing and putting on his best uniform, he reached for his normal military socks and shoes, then remembered the old woman's gift.

I shall wear the pair proudly, he thought, stirred by the depth of the devotion that she displayed.

He retrieved the socks from their cardboard box and slipped them on, enjoying their feel against his skin. After stepping into his shoes, he left the room and walked downstairs with plans for conquest spinning around in his brain.

At the large round table he shook hands with everyone.

"I am so happy," he said, a very broad smile lighting up his face. "We shall soon start the march that leads us to victory."

They all stood and saluted him.

He sat down, ready to enjoy the breakfast feast that had been set out before him.

He leaned forward to get a butter-smeared biscuit.

A quick cry escaped Saad Nasur's lips before life fled his body, and his eyes opened wide as the screams of hell surrounded what was left of him.

An elderly woman sat quietly in a far corner of a bazaar near the center of ancient Tripoli, smiling, as she knitted another pair of soft, black socks.

I must hurry.

Oh, I do, as always, usually at night, the darkness shrouding my movements better than the daylight, turning me into some kind of vampirish figure living in the shadows of the lives of those around me.

I am being transferred to another location.

There is some possibility that in the present location my security has been compromised.

> *—There are some indications, Mouphas, that the current regime is not only not relenting in the way they view your situation, but, in order to*

101

gain strong public backing at this early stage in their rule, they are pressing ahead with the death sentence more strongly than before.

—Yes, we know that does sound rather impossible. How could matters be worse than the previous state of affairs? But you must remember as long as those degenerates, those members of the Ba'ath Party are in power, there is no hope of a genuinely better situation.

—Trust us, Mouphas — you are in the gravest danger yet....

How long will it be like this?

Saad Nasur is dead, yes — and part of me rejoices at that fact, so long yearned for by me, by many.

And yet I am still made to fear for my life.

There is but one explanation, of course.

Saad Nasur was simply the latest. And already one has risen from the masses to supplant him.

In the Middle East as a whole, not just in my fatherland, countless numbers of vicious men like him remain. They have been made so by their ancestry. They have inherited the very genes of generations, from Mohammed himself through to Sallamen and on to Khomeini.

They seem mad because of what they believe, because of the delusions imposed upon them by Islam — and what shame I feel that I ever partook of the brew it has concocted for millions of human beings enslaved by it.

How differently the history of the latter part of the twentieth century would have to be written!

Too much is *not* said these days for fear of offending some minority in the United States!

You mustn't step on the toes of the homosexuals, for example. And you mustn't offend the Hari Krishnis or the Hindis.

Or the Muslims.

The U.S. Constitution, which I have been studying for some time, mandates certain rights, for the homosexuals and the pornographers and the New Agers, and, yes, those terrorist-supporting Muslims. In America today the emphasis on personal rights has, in effect, perverted justice.

That is indeed something to consider...the mafia leader who is at large, who has not yet been sent to jail as punishment for his crimes; drug pushers who are put on trial but whose lawyers are clever enough to get the charges dismissed; the unrepentant rapist.

Am I encouraging civil disobedience? Am I coming in favor of vigilante groups prowling the streets of the United States of America?

Of course not. For that would be the scenario for a nightmare as bad as the conditions that would have brought it into existence.

But I *am* saying that something must be done to stop the onrushing incidences of violence by those who take the law into *their* hands.

Now *there* is a thought to stir up controversy, you can be sure of that, my readers!

But let me go on from there:

There will be no unrepentant homosexuals in heaven.

Nor any pornographers who have not shed the filth of their profession.

Nor the New Agers who deny the deity of Christ and assume a portion of that deity for themselves!

And no one, young or old, man or woman, who persists in being a Ku Klux Klan member.

And in the same way no unregenerate Muslim will ever stand before Almighty God except in terrible judgment before being cast into the lake of fire for all eternity.

In fact, even seemingly moral Western church-goers who trust in their own self-righteousness will be turned away.

Only one type of person will ever make it to heaven.

The Christian who is a Christian beyond just the assump-

tion of the label itself—the Christian who has accepted Jesus Christ as Savior and Lord!

I can say for certain that such words are *not* the stuff of some warped and inhumane bigotry, arising from the same source as anti-Semitism and racial hatred against blacks.

Those cold and cruel thought patterns are unwarranted! And they go directly against so much of what Scripture teaches.

Such thoughts come only from Satan himself, and there can be no valid claim to the contrary.

It is hard for me to believe that any Muslim who continues to follow the teachings of the Koran deserves even a modicum of respect.

Oh, I know there is likely to be an outcry against this sort of statement, an outcry rampant in the United States and elsewhere about prejudice, about civil rights, about judging others.

But the very essence of God's Word presents all that is necessary in order to view these demonically deluded individuals.

They are without Christ.

This must be said. It cannot be avoided in the name of

being nonjudgmental.

They are not only without Christ, but they reduce Him to the level of a second-rate prophet, one standing in a line with so many others.

They attempt to rob Him of His divinity. And in so doing, I believe they commit the one sin that cannot be forgiven — rejection of Jesus Christ.

How can there be devout Muslims in heaven? By the words of Jesus Christ I must say no, there cannot be, though I feel He would have me say it with sadness.

They will be stopped at the gates, as it were, and turned back.

Yet for now they are still dangerous.

But it is madness coupled with the manipulation of Satan himself, and so they are able to do the worst sort of damage.

Every Muslim who has not unequivocally rejected the calls for *jihad* is a potential enemy of everyone else.

Even those Muslims who have been turning their backs on the Saad Nasurs of their world continue to be *possible* time bombs because of Mohammed, the one to whom they pay homage, the very center of their faith, the very architect of all that they believe.

I know, of course, since I have been there with them.

I have joined the livid crowds. I have added my voice to the din.

And because I turned away, because I seek now to tell the abysmal truths about their abysmal way of life, they are out to destroy me.

I must regard *any* Muslim as someone who may have a hidden dagger, with the willingness to use it.

I can take no water from a Muslim hand because that hand may have laced it with a tiny pill or some flecks of powder.

I must survey each crowd before me, whatever the size, from the window of an apartment or a passing car and wonder who among the multitude has spotted me and is readying a small bomb or a grenade or a Molotov cocktail, thinking they will be honoring Allah in the process.

They want what I must keep as long as possible.

My life.

It is not theirs to take.

It is mine to give, to give for the human race, to try and alert the world to truths without which no one will be safe.

And I choose to give this life for others, if I must.

I do this because of the One who taught me how, who taught me what I desperately needed to learn — but at the expense of His own mortal life, His pain, His shed and cleansing blood — who taught me that it is better to give up one's life if, by keeping that life, we relegate Him to some back corner of our daily existences, playing it safe with our flesh, smug perhaps in our immortality.

I follow His example, you know. I must be prepared to walk in His steps down whatever path has been decreed.

Someday all Christians will have to take a stand. Someday it may well be a battle in the streets against hordes of charging Muslims who are not afraid of death — because if they die while fighting infidels, Allah has guaranteed them rewards beyond comprehension in his kingdom.

Saad, Saad, you think there is victory when this body of mine falls for the last time? And your puppets slink away in the shadows, assuming success?

Oh, Saad, if only your shouts from hell could be heard by them and the others who hold you high in their minds and follow you in their hearts.

But you cannot be heard, Saad, your words not reaching beyond the boundaries of your damnation.

This is Mouphas Fakarian's publisher again. I must add the final words, words that my dear, dear friend himself surely would have written if he had remained alive just a short while longer.

For too long, it seems, American men, women and children have had little to fear on the turf they call home.

For too long they have been surrounded by their huge oceans, insulated from any kind of suffering on their domestic soil, and yet crying with such tears when the body bags start to roll in from a foreign field.

What if it — the war, the conflict, the invasion, whatever

the fashionable word of the moment — were three streets away in your own town and due on your block any minute?

For too long there has been war in Europe and South Africa and in the Pacific and throughout Central and South America. Yes, Pearl Harbor was attacked, but at that time Hawaii was not a state. At that time the islands seemed just that — remote, separated from the mainland by thousands of miles of water, and people did react: "What a tragedy! What treachery! What devastation! But, thank God, it didn't happen here!"

But on American soil there are now several targets. If the terrorist squads themselves weren't sure of the best targets, the electronic media journalists would surely tell them, even going as far as drawing maps and diagrams.

Here is where the Muslim penchant for revenge will be felt in the spread of insane acts — men, women and children slaughtered by the scores as planes crash or are blown up in midair, as bus terminals are reduced to rubble, as seats of government are hit by sophisticated missiles, as supermarket aisles are clogged with more than broken bottles of ketchup.

Americans have never had to face such a nightmare.

Americans have grown up thinking of their country as a safe haven.

No longer.

"And don't bother to ask for mercy," the Muslim terrorists will say. "If you do, American Satans, you will be viewed as fools as well as the devils you are. You will not receive mercy from us.

"You bombed too many air-raid shelters.

"You destroyed too many residential areas.

"You stained too much of our fatherland with the blood of our strong young men and our helpless children."

Yes, it is coming.

It is coming in a month perhaps, in a year, whenever the plans of faceless terrorists are finalized.

And then you will see....

You will see that the words I speak are not those of a condemned man ranting in the shadows of his mad imaginings.

Your blood will join mine, in a common human pool of those victims of a malevolent force named Islam, sprung loose from the darkest corners of a literal place called hell.

This time, you can be sure, it won't be the mindless puppets of the deposed Dark Knight.

At least, I should say, not *that* Dark Knight, not Saad Nasur.

There is another.

The one who replaced Saad.

The successor to a tyrant who may have his own imbalances guiding him. What little I have found out gives me no basis for the least bit of optimism.

He is waiting, this new one.

This time perhaps the leader of my tormented land may emerge as the feared Antichrist, though one must admit that the same was suspected of Saad Nasur. True, he was assassinated; yet he was not resurrected. And Saad did not become the martyr he had hoped to be in the event of his death.

Then again, the one who now sits on the throne may not be anything other than what he seems at the moment, simply another in the long history of Muslim despots.

Either way, Antichrist or not, the new man — if that can be said of such creatures as this — wants the same things as Saad did. The very same things, even though he rode in on a horse named Liberation.

Americans cannot cope with such deception. Not that Americans are incapable of some use of the technique, else there would never have been Watergate or any of the other scandals that have littered the political landscape for many years in the United States.

But deception in the Middle East has been practiced for *centuries*.

The Americans are quite new at it. They haven't learned to refine the art, shall we say, with quite as much adeptness as your average Muslim. When a Saad Nasur comes on the scene — men who are brilliant at what they do — at no time must any of them be taken for granted, as though to say, "Well, we handled Nasur well enough," and implying that the next in line will be a pushover.

It is true that some lessons were learned through the confrontation with Saad. Any new war can be fought with greater efficiency. But presidents and generals and diplomats must realize they are not the only ones capable of learning. You see, Muslim despots can be extremely cruel and vengeful. But they are not stupid. No, not that.

And he must be feared, this one, or the one after him, or the one after that, feared because of the inbred tendency of each Muslim tyrant to become more ferocious than the last.

Consider this, please: Can the evil of Saad Nasur be compared to anything for which Gamal Abdel Nasser was responsible? The two seem to be from altogether different species, do they not?

There can be no complacency. No true Muslim who follows the Koran can be completely trusted. Can the sole of a shoe trust the dirt of the road to keep it clean?

If you are not one of them, then you are *anathema*, incarnations of evil. Jews or Christians, atheists or agnostics — according to the Koran, all must be scourged from the face of this planet.

Be vigilant, I say.

A Muslim doesn't have to be the Antichrist to bring all manner of destruction down around us.

Do not be deceived by alliances.

Do not say, "Well, they helped us during the last war," because it is already yesterday of which we speak. And the yesterdays of the Muslim world are strewn with the rubble of one-time friends, of allies side by side but only for a fleeting instant, drowned in the bloody tumult of today's infamy.

You see, my readers — none of whom I will be able to meet this side of glory, and for that I am the poorer — if this newest devil-in-disguise, like all the others among the shifting sand dunes of the Middle East, has his way, it won't be John the Baptist's head on a platter the next time.

EPILOGUE

So there it is, the sum total of Mouphas Fakarian's legacy, some pieces of paper in a folder for a book he did not quite complete before he died.

And how did my friend die?

He was in church during a Sunday evening service. He was disguised with a beard, and he wore a pair of dark sunglasses. His head was shaved of all hair.

No one should have known, of course.

But they did, these fanatical Muslims.

And they machine-gunned Mouphas Fakarian to death. Nearly a hundred bullets were found in his body.

Murdered in a church as he worshipped his Savior.

Murdered along with everyone else in the sanctuary.

No witnesses were left.

The American authorities wondered how the terrorist group responsible could ever have found out.

How could this have been?

They came to the only conclusion possible. Someone on the inside tipped off the murderers of this man, of the others.

I understand that an intensive investigation has begun.

I have dialed the phone number of my undercover contact at the FBI, giving the agent who answered the phone my special code word.

"I have the package," I told him. "You must stop by immediately."

"Yes," he replied. "Give me fifteen minutes."

"Fine," I told him. "Tell the others I have added a special note of my own. Tell them it is authentic."

I hung up the receiver and just stood there in the middle of my office.

"Oh, Mouphas!" I cried aloud.

This is the end of my note. I hold now, with my free hand, a snub-nosed revolver. I am unable to live another moment with what I have done, unable to face the truth about myself, about the world in which I live. They can get to anybody, you know, anybody.

They can come in and take over that person's very soul.

They work through their human automatons, from the halls of the Congress to the Houses of

Parliament, from Honolulu and Anchorage and Atlanta, from anywhere to everywhere — even the office of a certain publisher of books.

I am so sorry, Mouphas — my friend, my dear friend.

So very sorry.

AFTERWORD

It could be said that the foregoing material, though fiction, is based to a great extent upon fact.

It could be said that many of the expressed emotions are exceptionally heated and accusatory.

But then we have our Lord as a model in the latter regard, don't we? Who can forget that portion of Scripture in which Christ is depicted as throwing the money changers out of the temple?

He saw conditions that were intolerable. And He acted accordingly, even violently.

When Jesus stood before the religious leaders of that time and place, He judged them by calling them whited sepulchers on the outside — but full of dead men's bones inside, all dusty and dirty and smelly.

Should we *ever* do less about the conditions of today?

For once the United States stood firm, and effectively, against someone like this fictional character of Saad Nasur.

But what about the other despicables? It could be hoped that they will be blacklisted by the United States, by other governments, that they will be cut off until they either repent or someone worthier than they governs the ancient lands.

It is likely that diplomacy will shield them, will allow them some face-saving gesture, and they will once again hold their heads high — though how they could ever legitimately do so from now on is beyond most of us, I suspect.

Are these Muslims as dangerous, as maniacal, as has been graphically portrayed in *Dark Knight*? If they are true to their beliefs, as interpreted by Muslim fundamentalists, the only answer is yes.

Is there a real possibility that the violence meted out by policemen across the United States has anything to do with the infiltration of their departments by dedicated neo-Nazis?

Call it coincidence or not, but the rise of the "skinhead" movement, the burgeoning instances of hate mail and bombs sent to judges, and other clear-cut proofs that *something* is going on — these *are* happening on a parallel track, shall we say.

Interesting, these times in which we live — frightening on one level, but altogether wonderful on another.

We just may be witnessing the playing out of a drama that was foretold thousands of years ago.

But we need not fear, as the Word of God assures us. Those who would take our bodies cannot touch our souls. And in the stunning and transcendent realization of that crucial fact lies the peace that passes all understanding.

Praise God.

Praise His holy name.

For now. For eternity.